Favorite
Just So Stories

H.B. VESTAL

Favorite
Just So Stories

by *Rudyard Kipling*
Illustrated by *H. B. Vestal*

GROSSET & DUNLAP • **Publishers** • **NEW YORK**
A FILMWAYS COMPANY

ISBN: 0-448-12691-5 (Paperback Edition)
ISBN: 0-448-03204-X (Library Edition)
Library of Congress Catalog Card Number: 76-14697

HOW THE WHALE
GOT HIS TINY THROAT

SOME stories are meant to be read quietly and some stories are meant to be told aloud. Some stories are only proper for rainy mornings, and some for long, hot afternoons when one is lying in the open, and some stories are bedtime stories. All the Blue Skalallatoot stories are morning tales (I do not know why, but that is what Effie says). All the stories about Orvin Sylvester Woodsey, the left-over New England fairy who did not think it well-seen to fly, and who used patent labor-saving devices instead of charms, are afternoon stories, because they were generally told in the shade of the woods. You could alter and change these tales as much as you pleased; but in the evening there were stories meant to put Effie to sleep, and you were not allowed to alter those by one single little word. They had to be told just so, or Effie would wake up and put back the missing sentence. So at last they came to be like charms, all three of them — the whale tale, the camel tale, and the rhinoceros tale. Of course little people are not alike, but I think if you catch some Effie rather tired and rather sleepy at the end of the day, and if you begin in a low voice and tell the tales precisely as I have written them down, you will find that Effie will presently curl up and go to sleep.

Now, this is the first tale, and it tells how the whale got his tiny throat:

Once upon a time there was a whale, and he lived in the sea and he ate fishes. He ate the starfish and the garfish, and the crab and the dab, and the plaice and the dace, and the skate and his mate, and the mackerel and the pickereel, and the really truly twirly-whirly eel. All the fishes he could find in all the sea he ate with his mouth — so! At last there was only one little fish left in all the sea, and he was an astute fish, and he swam a little behind the whale's right ear so as to be out of harm's way. Then the whale stood up on his tail and said, "I'm hungry." And the little 'stute fish said in a little 'stute voice, "Noble and generous Cetacean, have you ever tried Man?"

"No," said the whale. "What is it like?"

"Nice," said the little 'stute fish. "Nice, but nubbly."

"Then fetch me a dozen," said the whale, and he made the sea froth up with his tail.

"One at a time is enough," said the 'stute fish. "If you swim to latitude 41.42, longitude 36.37 (that is magic), you will find sitting *on* a raft, *in* the middle of the sea, with nothing on but a pair of blue canvas breeches, a pair of suspenders (you must *not* forget the suspenders), and a jackknife, one shipwrecked mariner, who, it is only fair to tell you, is a man of infinite-resource-and-sagacity."

So the whale swam and swam to latitude 41.42, longitude 36.37, as fast as he could swim; and *on* a raft, *in* the middle of the sea, *with* nothing to wear except a pair of blue canvas breeches, a pair of suspenders (you must particularly remember the suspenders) and a jackknife, he found one single, solitary shipwrecked mariner trailing his toes in the water. (He had his mother's leave to paddle, or else he would never have done it, because he was a man of infinite-resource-and-sagacity.)

Then the whale opened his mouth back and back and back till it nearly touched his tail; and he swallowed the shipwrecked mariner, and

the raft he was sitting on, and his blue canvas breeches, and the suspenders (which you *must* not forget), and the jackknife — he swallowed them all down into his warm, dark inside cupboards, and then he smacked his lips — so, and turned round three times on his tail.

But as soon as the mariner, who was a man of infinite-resource-and-sagacity, found himself in the whale's warm, dark inside cupboards, he hopped and he jumped and he thumped and he bumped, and he pranced and he danced, and he banged and he clanged, and he leaped and he creeped, and he prowled and he howled, and he cried and he sighed, and

he crawled and he bawled, and he danced hornpipes where he shouldn't, and the whale felt very unhappy indeed. (*Have* you forgotten the suspenders?)

So he said to the 'stute fish, "This man is truly very nubbly, and, besides, he is making me hiccup. What shall I do?"

"Tell him to come out," said the 'stute fish. So the whale called down his own throat to the shipwrecked mariner, "Come out and behave yourself. I've got the hiccups."

"Nay — nay," said the mariner. "Not so, but far otherwise. Take me to my natal shore and the white-cliffs-of-Albion, and I'll think about it." And he began to dance again.

"You had better humor him," said the 'stute fish to the whale. "I ought to have warned you that he is a man of infinite-resource-and-sagacity."

So the whale swam and swam and swam, with both flippers and his tail, as hard as he could for the hiccups; and at last he saw the mariner's natal shore and the white-cliffs-of-Albion, and he rushed halfway up the beach, and opened his mouth wide and wide and wide, and said, "Change here for Winchester, Ashuelot, Nashua, Keene, and stations on the *Fitch*burg road." And just as he said "Fitch" the mariner walked out of his mouth. But while the whale had been swimming, the mariner, who was indeed a person of infinite-resource-and-sagacity, had taken his jack-knife and cut up the raft into a little square grating all running criss-cross, and he had tied it firm with his suspenders (*now* you know why you were not to forget the suspenders), and he dragged that grating good

11

and tight into the whale's throat, and there it stuck. Then he recited the following *Sloka,* which, as you have not heard it, I will now proceed to relate:

> By means of a grating
> I have stopped your ating.

For the mariner — he was also an Hi-ber-ni-an. And he stepped out on the shingle, and went home to his mother, who had given him leave to trail his toes in the water; and he married and lived happily ever afterward. So did the whale, but from that day on, the grating in his throat, which he could neither cough up nor swallow down, prevented him eating anything except very, very small fish; and that is the reason why whales nowadays never eat men or boys or little girls.

The 'stute fish went and hid himself in the mud under the doorsills of the Equator. He was afraid the whale might be angry with him.

The sailor took the jackknife home. He was wearing the blue canvas breeches when he walked out on the shingle. The suspenders were left behind, you see, to tie the grating with; and that is the end of *that* tale.

HOW THE CAMEL GOT HIS HUMP

OW this is the second tale, and it tells how the camel got his big hump.

In the beginning of years, when the world was so new and all, and the animals were just beginning to work for Man, there was a Camel, and he lived in the middle of a Howling Desert because he did not want to work. So he ate sticks and thorns and tamarisk and milkweed and prickles, most 'scruciating idle; and when anybody spoke to him he said, "Humph!" — just "Humph!" and no more.

Presently the Horse came to him one Monday morning, with a saddle on his back and a bit in his mouth, and said, "Camel, oh Camel, come out and trot like the rest of us."

"Humph!" said the Camel; and the Horse went away and told the Man.

Presently the Dog came to him, with a stick in his mouth, and said, "Camel, oh Camel, come and fetch and carry like the rest of us."

"Humph!" said the Camel; and the Dog went away and told the Man.

Presently the Ox came to him, with a yoke on his neck, and said, "Camel, oh Camel, come and plow like the rest of us."

"Humph!" said the Camel; and the Ox went away and told the Man.

At the end of the day the Man called the Horse and the Dog and the Ox together, and said, "Three, oh three, I'm very sorry for you, with the world so new and all; but that Humph-thing in the desert can't work or he would have been here by now, so I am going to leave him alone, and you must work double time to make up for it."

That made the Three very angry, with the world so new and all, and they held a palaver on the edge of the desert; and the Camel came chewing milkweed *most* 'scruciating idle, and laughed at them. Then he said, "Humph!" and went away again.

Presently there came along the Djinn in charge of All Deserts, rolling in a cloud of dust (Djinns always travel that way because it is Magic), and he stopped to palaver with the Three.

"Djinn of All Deserts," said the Horse, "*is* it right for any one to be idle, with the world so new and all?"

"Certainly not," said the Djinn.

"Well," said the Horse, "there's a thing in the middle of your desert with a long neck and long legs, and he hasn't done a stroke of work since Monday morning. He won't trot."

"Whew!" said the Djinn, whistling, "that's my camel, for all the gold in Arabia! What does he say about it?"

"He says 'Humph'" said the Dog, "and he won't fetch and carry."

"Did he say anything else?"

"Only 'Humph'; and he won't plow," said the Ox.

"Very good," said the Djinn. "I'll humph him if you will kindly wait a minute."

The Djinn rolled himself up in his dust-cloak, and took a bearing across the Desert, and found the Camel most 'scruciatingly idle, looking at his own reflection in a pool of water.

"Come hither, my tall friend," said the Djinn. "What's this I hear of your doing no work, with the world so new and all?"

"Humph!" said the Camel.

The Djinn sat down, with his chin in his hand, and began to think a Great Magic, while the Camel looked at his reflection in the pool of water.

"You've given the Three extra work ever since Monday morning, all on account of your 'scruciating idleness," said the Djinn. "Have you anything to say for yourself?"

"Humph!" said the Camel.

"You'll say that once too often," said the Djinn, and he went on thinking Magics, with his chin in his hand.

And the Camel said it again; but no sooner had he said it than he saw his back, that he was so proud of, puffing up and puffing up into a great big lollopping humph.

"Do you see that?" said the Djinn. "That's your very own humph that you've brought upon your very own self by not working. Today is Thursday, and you've done no work since Monday, when the work began. Now you are going to work."

16

"How can I" said the Camel, "with this humph on my back?"

"That's made a-purpose," said the Djinn, "all because you missed those three days. You will be able to work now for three days without eating, because you can live on your humph; and don't you ever say I never did anything for you. Come out of the desert and go to the Three, and behave. Humph, yourself!"

And the Camel humphed himself, humph and all, and went away to join the Three. And from that day to this the Camel always wears a humph (they call it "hump" now, not to hurt his feelings); but he has never yet caught up with the three days that he missed at the beginning of the world, and he has never yet learned to behave.

HOW THE LEOPARD
GOT HIS SPOTS

IN THE days when everybody started fair, Best Beloved, the Leopard lived in a place called the High Veldt. 'Member it wasn't the Low Veldt, or the Bush Veldt, or the Sour Veldt, but the 'sclusively bare hot shiny High Veldt, where there was sand and sandy-colored rock and 'sclusively tufts of sandy-yellowish grass. The Giraffe and the Zebra and the Eland and the Koodoo and the Hartebeest lived there and they were 'sclusively sandy-yellow-brownish all over; but the Leopard, he was the 'sclusivest, sandiest-yellowest-brownest of them all—a grayish-yellowish, catty-shaped kind of beast, and he matched the 'sclusively yellowish-grayish-brownish color of the High Veldt to one hair. That was very bad for the Giraffe and the Zebra and the rest of them; for he would lie down by a 'sclusively yellowish-grayish-brownish stone or clump of grass, and when the Giraffe or the Zebra or the Eland or the Koodoo or the Bush-Buck or the Bonte Buck came by he would surprise them out of their jumpsome lives. And, also, there

18

was an Ethiopian with bows and arrows (a 'sclusively grayish-brownish-yellowish man he was then), who lived on the High Veldt with the Leopard; and the two used to hunt together — the Ethiopian with his bows and arrows, and the Leopard 'sclusively with his teeth and claws — till the Giraffe and the Eland and the Koodoo and the Quagga and all the rest of them didn't know which way to jump, Best Beloved. They didn't indeed.

After a long time — people lived forever so long in those days — they learned to avoid anything that looked like a Leopard or an Ethiopian; and bit by bit — the Giraffe began it (his legs were longest) — they went away from the High Veldt. They scuttled for days and days and days till they came to a great forest, 'sclusively full of trees and bushes and stripy, speckly, patchy shadows, and there they hid, and after another long time, what with standing half in the shade and half out of it, and what with the slippery-slidy shadows of the trees falling on them, the

19

Giraffe grew blotchy and the Zebra grew stripy and the Eland and the Koodoo grew darker with little gray lines on their backs like bark on a tree trunk; and though you could hear them and smell them you could very seldom see them, and then only when you knew precisely where to look. They had a beautiful time in the 'sclusively speckly-spickly shadows of the forest, while the Leopard and the Ethiopian ran about all over the 'sclusively grayish-yellowish-reddish High Veldt wondering where all their breakfasts and their dinners and their teas had gone. At last they were so hungry that they ate rats and beetles and rock rabbits, the Leopard and the Ethiopian, and then they had big tummy-ache, and then they met

Baviaan — the dog-headed barking Baboon, who is quite the wisest animal in all South Africa.

Said Leopard to Baviaan (and it was a very hot day), "Where has all the game gone?"

And Baviaan winked. *He* knew.

Said the Ethiopian to Baviaan, "Can you tell me the present habitat of the aboriginal Fauna?"

And Baviaan winked. *He* knew.

Then said Baviaan, "The game has gone into other spots, and my advice to you, Leopard, is to go into other spots as soon as you can."

And the Ethiopian said, "That is all very fine, but I wish to know whither the aboriginal Fauna has migrated."

Then said Baviaan, "The aboriginal Fauna has joined the aboriginal Flora because it was high time for a change; and my advice to you, Ethiopian, is to change as soon as you can."

That puzzled the Leopard and the Ethiopian, but they set off to look for the aboriginal Flora, and presently, after ever so many days, they saw a great, high, tall forest full of tree trunks, all 'sclusively speckled and dotted and splashed and slashed and hatched and cross-hatched with shadows.

"What is this," said the Leopard, "that is so 'sclusively dark and so full of little pieces of light?"

"I don't know," said the Ethiopian, "but it ought to be the aboriginal Flora. I can smell Giraffe and I can hear Giraffe, but I can't see Giraffe."

"That's curious," said the Leopard. "I suppose it is because we have just come in out of the sunshine. I can smell Zebra and I can hear Zebra, but I can't see Zebra."

"Wait a bit," said the Ethiopian. "It's a long time since we've hunted 'em. Perhaps we've forgotten what they were like."

"Fiddle!" said the Leopard. "I remember them perfectly on the

High Veldt, especially their marrowbones. Giraffe is about seventeen feet high, of a 'sclusively fulvous golden-yellow from head to heel; and Zebra is about four and a half feet high of a 'sclusively gray-fawn color from head to heel."

"Umm," said the Ethiopian, looking into the speckly-spickly shadows of the aboriginal Flora. "Then they ought to show up in this dark place like ripe bananas in a smokehouse."

But they didn't. The Leopard and the Ethiopian hunted all day, and though they could smell them and hear them they never saw one of them.

"For goodness sake," said the Leopard at tea time, "let us wait till it gets dark. This daylight hunting is a perfect scandal."

So they waited till dark, and then the Leopard heard something breathing sniffily in the starlight that fell all stripy through the branches, and he jumped in the direction of the noise, and it smelled like Zebra and it felt like Zebra, and when he knocked it down it kicked like Zebra.

So he said, "Be quiet. This is much too serious for dumb-crambo. (He meant he wouldn't eat him up, Best Beloved.) I am going to sit on your head till morning, because there is something about you I don't understand."

Presently he heard a grunt and a crash and a scramble, and the Ethiopian called out, "I've caught a thing that I can't see. It smells like Giraffe and it kicks like Giraffe."

"Don't you trust it," said the Leopard. "Sit on its head till the morning — same as me."

So they sat down hard till morning-time and then Leopard said, "What have you at your end of the table, Brother?"

The Ethiopian scratched his head and said, "It ought to be 'sclusively a rich fulvous orange-tawny from head to heel, and it ought to be Giraffe, but it is covered all over with chestnut blotches. What have you at your end of the table, Brother?"

And the Leopard scratched his head and said, "It ought to be 'sclusively a delicate grayish fawn, and it ought to be Zebra, but it is covered all over with black and chestnut stripes. What in the world have you been doing to yourself, Zebra? Don't you know that if you were on the High Veldt I could see you ten miles off?"

"Yes," said the Zebra, "but this isn't the High Veldt. Can't you see?"

"I can now," said the Leopard. "But I couldn't all yesterday. How is it done?"

"Let us up," said the Zebra, "and we will show you."

They let the Zebra and the Giraffe get up; and the Zebra moved away to some little thorn-bushes where the sunlight fell all stripy, and the Giraffe moved off to some tall-ish trees where the shadows fell all blotchy.

"Now watch," said the Zebra and the Giraffe. "This is the way it's done. One — two — three! And where's your breakfast?"

Leopard stared and Ethiopian stared, but all they could see were stripy shadows and blotched shadows in the forest, but never a sign of Zebra or Giraffe. They had just walked off and hidden themselves in the shadowy forest.

"Hi!" said the Ethiopian. "That's a trick worth learning. Take a lesson by it, Leopard. You show up in this dark place like a bar of soap in a coal hod."

"Ho!" said the Leopard. "Would it surprise you very much to know that you show up in this dark place like a mustard-plaster on a sack of coals?"

"Well, calling names won't catch dinner," said the Ethiopian. "The long and the little of it is that we don't match our backgrounds. I'm going to take Baviaan's advice. He told me I ought to change, and as I've nothing to change except my skin I'm going to change that."

"What to?" said the Leopard, tremendously excited.

"To a nice working blackish-brownish color, with a little purple in it and a touch of slaty-blue. It will be the very thing for hiding in hollows and behind trees."

So he changed his skin then and there, and the Leopard was more excited than ever. He had never seen a man change his skin before.

"But what about me?" he said when the Ethiopian had worked his last little finger into his fine new black skin.

"You take Baviaan's advice, too. He told you to go into spots."

"So I did," said the Leopard. "I went into other spots as fast as I could. I went into this spot with you, and a lot of good it has done me."

"Oh," said the Ethiopian, "Baviaan didn't mean spots in South Africa. He meant spots on your skin."

"What's the use of that?" said the Leopard.

"Think of Giraffe," said the Ethiopian. "Or if you prefer stripes, think of Zebra. They find their spots and stripes give them perfect satisfaction."

"Umm," said the Leopard. "I wouldn't look like Zebra — not for anything."

"Well, make up your mind," said the Ethiopian, "because I'd hate to go hunting without you, but I must if you insist on looking like a sunflower in a back parlor."

"I'll take spots then," said the Leopard, "but don't make 'em too big. I wouldn't be like Giraffe — not for anything."

"I'll make 'em with the tips of my fingers," said the Ethiopian. "There's plenty black left on my skin still. Stand over!"

Then the Ethiopian put his five fingers close together and pressed them all over the Leopard, and wherever the five fingers touched they left five little black marks all close together. You can see them on any Leopard's skin you like, Best Beloved. Sometimes the fingers slipped and the marks got a little blurred, but if you look closely at any Leopard now, you will see that there are always five spots, off five fat, black finger-tips.

"Now you *are* a beauty!" said the Ethiopian. "You can lie out on the bare ground and look like a heap of pebbles. You can lie out on the naked rocks and look like a piece of pudding-stone. You can lie out on a leafy branch and look like sunshine, through the leaves; and you can lie right across the center of a path and look like nothing in particular. Think of that and purr!"

"But if I'm all this," said the Leopard, "why didn't you go spotty too?"

"Oh, plain black's best," said the Ethiopian. "Now come along and we'll see if we can't get even with Mr. One-two-three, where's your breakfast?"

So they went away and lived happily ever afterward, Best Beloved. That is all.

Oh, now and then you will hear grownups say, "Can the Ethiopian change his skin or the Leopard his spots?" I don't think grownups would keep on saying such an absurd thing if the Leopard and Ethiopian hadn't done it once — do you? But they will never do it again, Best Beloved. They are quite contented as they are.

HOW THE ELEPHANT
GOT HIS TRUNK

IN THE HIGH and Far-Off Times the Elephant, oh, Best Beloved, had no trunk. He had only a blackish, bulgy nose, as big as a boot, that he could wriggle about from side to side; but he could not pick up things with it. But there was one Elephant — a new Elephant — an Elephant's Child — who was full of 'satiable curtiosity, and that means he asked ever so many questions. And he lived in Africa, and he filled all Africa with his 'satiable curtiosities. He asked his aunt, the Ostrich, why her tail-feathers grew just so, and she spanked him with her hard claw. He asked his uncle, the Giraffe, what made his skin spotty, and his uncle, the Giraffe, spanked him with his hard, hard hoof. And still he was full of 'satiable curtiosity. He asked his other aunt, the Hippopotamus, why her eyes were red, and she spanked him with her hard, hard hoof; and he asked his other uncle, the Baboon, why melons tasted just so, and his other uncle, the Baboon, spanked him with his hard, hard paw. And still he was full of 'satiable curtiosity. He asked questions about everything that he saw, or heard, or felt, or smelled, or touched, and all his uncles and his aunts spanked him; and still he was full of 'satiable curtiosity.

One fine morning in the middle of the Precession of the Equinoxes, this 'satiable Elephant's Child asked a new fine question that he had never asked before. He asked, "What does the Crocodile have for dinner?" Then everybody said "Hush!" in a loud and dretful tone, and they spanked him immediately and directly.

By and by, when that was finished, he came upon Kolokolo Bird sitting in the middle of a wait-a-bit thorn and he said, "My father has spanked me and my mother has spanked me; all my aunts and uncles have spanked me for my 'satiable curtiosity; and still I want to know what the Crocodile has for dinner!"

Then Kolokolo Bird said, with a mournful cry, "Go to the banks of the great, gray-green, greasy Limpopo River all set about with fever-trees and find out."

That very next morning, when there was nothing left of the Equinoxes, because the Precession had gone by, this 'satiable Elephant's Child took a hundred pounds of bananas, and a hundred pounds of sugar cane, and seventeen melons, and said to all his families, "Good-by. I am going to the great, gray-green, greasy Limpopo River all set about with fever-trees to find out what the Crocodile has for dinner." And they all spanked him once more for luck, though he requested them most politely to abstain.

Then he went away, a little warm but not at all astonished, eating melons and throwing the rind about.

He went from Graham's town to Kimberley, and from Kimberley to Khama's Country, and from Khama's Country he went east by north, eating melons all the time, till at last he came to the banks of the great, gray-green, greasy Limpopo River all set about with fever-trees precisely as Kolokolo Bird had said.

Now you must know and understand, oh, Best Beloved, that till that very week, and day, and hour, and minute, this 'satiable Elephant's Child had never seen a Crocodile and did not know what one was like. It was all his 'satiable curtiosity.

The first thing he found was a

Bi - Colored - Python - Rock - Snake curled round a rock.

"'Scuse me," said the Elephant's Child most politely, "but have you seen such a thing as a Crocodile in these promiscuous parts?"

"Have I seen a Crocodile?" said the Bi-Colored-Python-Rock-Snake, in a voice of dretful scorn. "What will you ask me next?"

"'Scuse me," said the Elephant's Child, "but could you kindly tell me what he has for dinner?"

Then the Bi-Colored-Python-Rock-Snake uncoiled himself from the rock and spanked the Elephant's Child with his hard, hard tail.

"That is odd," said the Elephant's Child, "because my father and my mother, and my uncle and my aunt, not to mention my other aunt, the Hippopotamus, and my other uncle, the Baboon, have all spanked me for my 'satiable curtiosity — and I suppose this is the same thing."

So he said good-by very politely to the Bi-Colored-Python-Rock-Snake, and helped to coil him up on the rock again, and went on, a little warm but not at all astonished, eating melons and throwing the rind about till he trod on what he thought was a log at the very edge of the great, gray-green, greasy Limpopo

River all set about with fever-trees. But it was really the Crocodile, oh, Best Beloved, and the Crocodile winked one eye.

"'Scuse me," said the Elephant's Child most politely, "but do you happen to have seen a Crocodile in these promiscuous parts?"

Then the Crocodile winked the other eye and lifted half his tail out of the mud; and the Elephant's Child stepped back most politely, because he did not wish to be spanked again.

"Come hither, Little One," said the Crocodile. "Why do you ask such things?"

"'Scuse me," said the Elephant's Child most politely, "but my father has spanked me, my mother has spanked me; not to mention my aunt, the Ostrich, and my uncle, the Giraffe, who can kick ever so hard, as well as my other aunt, the Hippopotamus, and my other uncle, the Baboon, *and* including the Bi-Colored-Python-Rock-Snake just up the bank who spanks harder than any of them; and so, if it's quite all the same to you, I don't want to be spanked any more."

"Come hither, Little One," said the Crocodile, "for I am the Crocodile," and he wept Crocodile tears to show it was quite true.

Then the Elephant's Child grew all breathless, and panted and kneeled down on the bank and said, "You are the very person I have been looking for all these long days. Will you please tell me what you have for dinner?"

"Come hither, Little One," said the Crocodile, "and I'll whisper."

Then the Elephant's Child, very excited and breathing hard, put his head down close to the Crocodile's musky, tusky mouth, and the Crocodile caught him by his little nose, which up to that very week, day, hour and minute, was no bigger than a boot, though much more useful.

"I think," said the Crocodile, and he said it between his teeth like this, "I think today we will begin with Elephant's Child!"

At this, oh, Best Beloved, the Elephant's Child was much annoyed, and he said, speaking through his nose like this, "Led go! You are hurtig be!"

Then the Bi-Colored-Python-Rock-Snake scuffled down from the bank and said, "My young friend, if you do not now, immediately and instantly, pull as hard as ever you can, it is my opinion that your acquaintance in the large-pattern leather ulster (and by this he meant the Crocodile) will jerk you into yonder limpid stream before you can say Jack Robinson." Bi-Colored-Python-Rock-Snakes always talk this way.

Then the Elephant's Child sat back on his little haunches, and pulled, and pulled, and pulled, and his nose began to stretch. And the Crocodile floundered into the water, making it all creamy with great sweeps of his tail, and *he* pulled, and pulled, and pulled. And the Elephant's Child's nose kept on stretching, and the Elephant's Child spread all his little four legs and pulled, and pulled, and pulled; and his nose kept on stretching, and the Crocodile threshed his tail like an oar, and *he* pulled, and pulled, and pulled, and at each pull the Elephant's Child's nose grew longer and longer — and it hurt him hijjus!

Then the Elephant's Child felt his legs slipping, and he said through his nose, which was now nearly five feet long, "This is too buch for be!"

Then the Bi-Colored-Python-Rock-Snake came down from the bank and knotted himself in a double clove-hitch round the Elephant's Child's hind legs and said, "Rash and inexperienced traveler, we will now seriously devote ourselves to a little hard pulling, because if we do not it is my impression that yonder self-propelling man-of-war with the armor-plated upper deck (and by this, oh, Best Beloved, he meant the Crocodile) will permanently vitiate your future career."

That is the way all Bi-Colored-Python-Rock-Snakes talk.

So he pulled, and the Elephant's Child pulled, and the Crocodile pulled, but the Elephant's Child and the Bi-Colored-Python-Rock-Snake pulled hardest, and at last the Crocodile let go of the Elephant's Child's nose with a plop that you could hear all up and down the Limpopo.

Then the Elephant's Child sat down most hard and sudden, but first he was careful to say, "Thank you," to the Bi-Colored-Python-Rock-Snake, and next he was kind to his nose and wrapped it all up in cool banana leaves and hung it in the great, gray-green, greasy Limpopo to cool.

"What are you doing that for?" said the Bi-Colored-Python-Rock-Snake.

"'Scuse me," said the Elephant's Child, "but my nose is out of shape and I am waiting for the swelling to go down."

"Then you will have to wait a long time," said the Bi-Colored-Python-Rock-Snake. "Some people do not know what is good for them."

The Elephant's Child sat there three days, waiting for his nose to get well. But it never grew any shorter, and besides it made him squint. For, oh, Best Beloved, you will see and understand that the Crocodile had pulled it out into a really truly trunk, same as all Elephants have today.

At the end of the third day a fly came and stung him on the shoulder, and instantly he lifted up his trunk and hit that fly dead with the end of it.

"'Vantage number one!" said the Bi-Colored-Python-Rock-Snake. "You couldn't have done that with a mere-smear nose. Try and eat a little now."

Before he thought what he was doing the Elephant's Child put out his trunk and plucked a large bundle of grass, dusted it clean against his fore legs and stuffed it into his own mouth.

"'Vantage number two!" said the Bi-Colored-Python-Rock-Snake. "You couldn't have done that with a mere-smear nose. Don't you think the sun is hot here?"

"It is," said the Elephant's Child, and, before he thought what he was doing, he scooped up a lump of mud from the banks of the great, gray-green, greasy Limpopo and slapped it on his head where it made a cool mudcap, all trickly behind his ears.

"'Vantage number three!" said the Bi-Colored-Python-Rock-Snake. "You couldn't have done that with a mere-smear nose. Now how do you feel about being spanked again?"

"'Scuse me," said the Elephant's Child, "but I should not like it at all."

"How would you like to spank somebody?" said the Bi-Colored-Python-Rock-Snake.

"I should like it very much indeed," said the Elephant's Child.

"Well," said the Bi-Colored-Python-Rock-Snake, "you will find that new nose of yours very useful to spank people with."

"Thank you," said the Elephant's Child, "I'll remember that; and now I think I'll go home to my families, and try it."

So the Elephant's Child went home across Africa, frisking and whisking his trunk. When he wanted fruit to eat he pulled it down from a tree, instead of waiting for it to fall as he used to do. When he wanted grass he plucked it up from the ground, instead of going on his knees as he used to do. When the flies bit him he broke off the branch of a tree and used it as a fly-whisk; and he made himself a new, cool, slushy mud-cap whenever the sun was hot. When he felt lonely walking through Africa he sang to himself down his trunk, and the noise was louder than

40

several brass bands. He went especially out of his way to find a Hippopotamus (she was no relation of his), and he spanked her very hard to make sure that the Bi-Colored-Python-Rock-Snake had spoken the truth about his new trunk. The rest of the time he picked up the melon rinds that he had dropped on his way to the Limpopo — for he was a Tidy Pachyderm.

One evening he came back to all his families and he coiled up his trunk and said, "How do you do?" They were glad to see him and immediately said, "Come here and be spanked for your 'satiable curtiosity."

"Pooh," said the Elephant's Child. "I don't think you peoples know anything about spanking, but *I* do and I'll show you."

Then he uncurled his trunk and knocked two of his brothers head over heels.

"Oh, Bananas!" said they. "Where did you learn that trick and what have you done to your nose?"

"I got a new one from the Crocodile on the bank of the great, gray-green, greasy Limpopo River," said the Elephant's Child. "I asked him what he had for dinner and he gave me this to keep."

"It looks very ugly," said the Baboon.

"It does," said the Elephant's Child. "But it's very useful," and he picked up his other uncle, the Baboon, by one leg and hove him into a bees' nest.

Then that bad Elephant's Child spanked all his families for a long time till they were very warm and greatly astonished. He pulled out his Ostrich Aunt's tail-feathers, and he caught his uncle, the Giraffe, by the hind leg and dragged him through a thorn bush; and he shouted at his other aunt, the Hippopotamus, and blew bubbles into her ear when she was sleeping in the water after meals, but he never let any one touch Kolokolo Bird.

In the end, things grew so bad that all his families went off one by one to the banks of the great, gray-green, greasy Limpopo River to borrow new noses from the Crocodile. When they came back everything started fair; and ever since that day, oh, Best Beloved, all the Elephants you will ever see, besides all those that you won't, have trunks precisely like the trunk of the 'satiable Elephant's Child.

THE BEGINNING OF THE ARMADILLOS

THIS, oh, Best Beloved, is another story of the High and Far-Off Times. In the very middle of those times was a Stickly-Prickly Hedgehog, and he lived on the banks of the turbid Amazon, eating snails and things. And he had a friend, a Slow-Solid Tortoise, who lived on the banks of the turbid Amazon, eating lettuces and things. And so that was all right, Best Beloved. Do you see?

But also, and at the same time, in those High and Far-Off Days, there was a Painted Jaguar, and he lived on the banks of the turbid Amazon too; and he ate everything that he could catch. When he could not catch deer or monkeys he would eat frogs and beetles; and when he could not catch frogs and beetles he went to his mother and she told him how to eat hedgehogs and tortoises.

She said to him ever so many times, graciously waving her tail, "My son, when you find a hedgehog you must drop him into the water, and then he will uncoil; and when you catch a tortoise you must scoop him out of his shell with your paw." And so that was all right, Best Beloved.

One beautiful night on the banks of the turbid Amazon, Painted Jaguar found Stickly-Prickly Hedgehog and Slow-Solid Tortoise under the trunk of a fallen tree. They could not run away, and so Stickly-Prickly curled himself up into a ball, and Slow-Solid Tortoise drew in his head and feet into his shell as far as they would go.

"Now attend to me," said Painted Jaguar, "because this is very important. My mother said that when I meet a hedgehog, I am to drop him into the water and then he will uncoil; and when I meet a tortoise I am to scoop him out of his shell with my paw. Now, which of you——"

"Are you sure?" said Stickly-Prickly Hedgehog. "Are you quite sure? Perhaps she said that when you uncoil a tortoise you must shell him out of the water with a scoop, and when you paw a hedgehog you must drop him."

"Are you sure?" said Slow-Solid Tortoise. "Are you quite sure? Perhaps she said that when you water a hedgehog you must drop him into your paw, and when you meet a tortoise you shell him till he uncoils."

"I don't think it was at all like that," said Painted Jaguar, but he felt a little puzzled. "Say it again more distinctly."

"When you scoop water with your paw you uncoil him with a hedgehog," said Stickly-Prickly. "Remember that, because it's important."

"But," said the Tortoise, "when you paw your meat you drop it into a tortoise with a scoop. Why can't you understand?"

"You are making my head ache," said Painted Jaguar, "and besides, I didn't want your advice at all. I only wanted to know which of you is Hedgehog and which is Tortoise."

"I shan't tell you," said Stickly-Prickly. "But you can scoop me out of my shell if you like."

"Aha!" said Painted Jaguar. "Now I know you're Tortoise. You thought I wouldn't! Take that!" Painted Jaguar darted out his paddy paw just as Stickly-Prickly curled himself up, and Jaguar's paw was filled with prickles. Worse than that he knocked Stickly-Prickly away and away into the woods and the bushes where it was too dark to find him. Then he put his paddy paw into his mouth, and, of course, the prickles hurt him more than ever. As soon as he could speak he said, "Aha! Now I know he isn't Tortoise at all. But" — then he scratched his head — "how do I know that this other is Tortoise?"

"But I *am* Tortoise," said Slow-Solid. "Your mother was quite right. She said that you were to scoop me out of my shell with your paw. Begin."

"You didn't say she said that a minute ago," said Painted Jaguar, sucking the prickles out of his paddy paw. "You said she said something quite different."

"Well, suppose you say that I said that she said something quite different, I don't see that it makes any difference, because if she said what you said I said she said, it's just the same as if I said what she said she said. Of course, if you think she said that you were to uncoil me with a scoop, instead of pawing me into drops with a shell, I can't help that, can I?"

"But you said you wanted to be scooped out of your shell with my paw," said Painted Jaguar.

"If you'll think again I didn't say anything of the kind. I said that your mother said that you were to scoop me out of my shell."

"What will happen if I do?" said the Jaguar very cautiously.

"I don't know, because I've never been scooped out of my shell before; but I tell you, honestly, if you want to see me swim away, you've only got to drop me into the water."

"I don't believe it," said Painted Jaguar. "You've mixed up all the things my mother told me to do till I don't know whether I'm on my head or my painted tail, and now you come and tell me something I can understand, and I don't trust you one little bit. My mother told me that I was to drop one of you two into the water, and as you seem so anxious to be dropped, I think you don't want to be dropped. Now jump into the turbid Amazon, and be quick about it."

"I warn you, your mother won't be pleased. Don't say I didn't tell you," said Slow-Solid.

"If you say another word about what my mother said —" the Jaguar answered, but he had not finished the sentence before Slow-

49

Solid quietly dived into the turbid Amazon, swam under water for a long way and came out on the bank where Stickly-Prickly was waiting for him.

"That was a very narrow escape," said Stickly-Prickly. "I don't like Painted Jaguar. What did you tell him you were?"

"I told him I was a truthful Tortoise, but he wouldn't believe it. Now he's gone to tell his mother. Listen to him!"

They could hear Painted Jaguar roaring up and down among the trees and the bushes by the side of the turbid Amazon.

"Son, son!" said his mother ever so many times, graciously waving her tail. "What have you been doing that you shouldn't have done?"

"I tried to scoop something that said it was a Tortoise out of its shell with my paw, and my paw is full of per-rickles," said Painted Jaguar.

"Son, son!" said his mother ever so many times, graciously waving her tail. "By the prickles on your paddy paw I see that must have been a Hedgehog. You should have dropped him into the water."

"I did that with another one, and he said he was a Tortoise, and I didn't believe him, and it was quite true, and he has dived, and he won't come up again, and I haven't anything at all to eat, and I think we had better find lodgings somewhere else. They are too clever on the turbid Amazon for poor me!"

"Son, son!" said his mother ever so many times, graciously waving her tail. "Now attend to me and remember what I say. A Hedgehog curls himself up into a ball and his prickles stick out every which way at once. By this you may know the Hedgehog."

"I don't like this old lady one little bit," said Stickly-Prickly, under the shadow of a large leaf. "I wonder what else she knows."

"A Tortoise can't curl himself up," Mother Jaguar went on, ever so many times, graciously waving her tail. "He only draws his head and legs into his shell. By this you may know the Tortoise."

"I don't like this old lady at all — at all," said Slow-Solid Tortoise. "Even Speckly Jaguar can't forget those directions. It's a great pity that you can't swim, Stickly-Prickly."

"Don't talk to me," said Stickly-Prickly. "Just think how much better it would be if you could curl up. This *is* a mess! Listen to Painted Jaguar."

Painted Jaguar was sitting on the banks of the turbid Amazon, sucking prickles out of his paws and saying to himself:

> "Can't curl, but can swim —
>   Slow-Solid, that's him!
> Curls up but can't swim,
>   Stickly-Prickly, that's him!"

"He'll never forget that this month of Sundays," said Stickly-Prickly. "Hold up my chin, Slow-Solid. I'm going to try to learn to swim."

"Excellent!" said Slow-Solid, and he held up Stickly-Prickly's chin, while Stickly-Prickly kicked in the water of the turbid Amazon.

"You'll make a fine swimmer yet," said Slow-Solid. "Now, not to be behindhand, if you can unlace my back-plates a little, I'll see what I can do toward curling up."

Stickly-Prickly helped to unlace Tortoise's back-plates, so that by twisting and straining Slow-Solid actually managed to curl up a tiddy wee bit.

"Excellent!" said Stickly-Prickly. "But I shouldn't do any more just now. It's making you black in the face. Kindly lead me into the water once more and I'll practice that side stroke which you say is so easy."

"Excellent!" said Slow-Solid. "A little more practice will make you a regular Gangetic Porpoise. Now, if I may trouble you to unlace my back- and front-plates, two holes, I'll try that fascinating bend that you say is so easy. Won't Painted Jaguar be surprised!"

"Excellent!" said Stickly-Prickly, all wet from the turbid Amazon. "I declare, I shouldn't know you from one of my own family. Two holes, I think you said. A little more expression, please, and don't grunt quite so much or Painted Jaguar may hear us. When you've finished I want to try that long dive which you say is so easy. Won't Painted Jaguar be surprised?"

"Excellent!" said Slow-Solid. "A little more attention to holding your breath and you will be able to keep house at the bottom of the turbid Amazon. Now I'll try that exercise of wrapping my hind legs around my ears which you say is so peculiarly comfortable. Won't Painted Jaguar be surprised?"

"Excellent!" said Stickly-Prickly. "But it's straining your back-plates a little. They are all overlapping now instead of lying side by side."

"Oh, that's the result of exercise," said Slow-Solid. "I've noticed that your prickles seem to be melting one into another, and that you're growing to look rather more like a pine cone, and less like a chestnut burr, than you used to."

"Am I?" said Stickly-Prickly. "That's the effect of soaking in the water. Oh, won't Painted Jaguar be surprised!"

They continued their exercises, each helping the other, till morning came, and when the sun was high they rested and dried themselves, when they saw that they were both of them quite different from what they had been.

"Stickly-Prickly," said Tortoise after breakfast, "I am not what I was yesterday, but I think I may yet amuse Painted Jaguar."

"That was the very thing I was thinking just now," said Stickly-Prickly. "I think scales are a tremendous improvement on prickles — to say nothing of being able to swim. Oh, won't Painted Jaguar be surprised! Let's go and find him."

By and by they found Painted Jaguar still nursing his paddy paw that had been hurt the night before. He was so astonished that he fell three times backward over his own painted tail without stopping.

"Good morning!" said Stickly-Prickly. "And how is your mamma this morning?"

"She is quite well, thank you," said Painted Jaguar, "but you must forgive me if I do not at this precise moment recall your name."

"That's unkind of you," said Stickly-Prickly, "seeing that this time yesterday you tried to scoop me out of my shell with your paw."

"But you hadn't any shell. It was all prickles," said Speckly Jaguar. "Just look at my paw."

"You told me to drop into the turbid Amazon and be drowned," said Slow-Solid. "Why are you so rude and forgetful today?"

"Don't you remember what your mother told you?" said Stickly-Prickly:

> "Can't curl, but can swim—
>   Stickly-Prickly, that's him!
>   Curls up, but can't swim,
>   Slow-Solid, that's him!"

Then they both curled themselves up and rolled round and round Painted Jaguar till his eyes turned cartwheels in his head.

Then he went to fetch his mother.

"Mother," he said, "there are two new animals in the woods today, and the one that you said couldn't swim, swims; and the one that you said couldn't curl up, curls; and they've gone shares in their prickles, I think, because both of them are scaly all over, instead of one being smooth and the other very prickly; and, besides that, they are rolling round and round in circles, and I don't feel comfy."

"Son, son!" said Mother Jaguar ever so many times, graciously waving her tail. "A hedgehog is a hedgehog, and can't be anything but a hedgehog; and a tortoise is a tortoise and can never be anything else."

"But it isn't a hedgehog, and it isn't a tortoise. It's a little bit of both, and I don't know its proper name."

"Nonsense!" said Mother Jaguar. "Everything has its proper name, I should call it 'armadillo' till I found out the real one. And I should leave it alone."

So Painted Jaguar did as he was told, especially about leaving them alone, but the curious thing is that from that day to this, oh, Best Beloved, no one on the banks of the turbid Amazon has ever called Stickly-Prickly

and Slow-Solid anything except Armadillo. There are hedgehogs and tortoises in other places, of course, but the real old and clever kind, with their scales lying lippety-lappety one over the other, like pine cone scales, that lived on the banks of the turbid Amazon in the High and Far-Off Days, are always called Armadillos because they were so clever. So that's all right, Best Beloved. Do you see?

THE SING~SONG OF OLD MAN KANGAROO

NOT always was the Kangaroo as we now behold him, but a different animal with four short legs. He was gray and he was woolly, and his pride was inordinate. He danced in a desert in the middle of Australia and he went to the Little God Nqa.

He went to Nqa at six before breakfast, saying, "Make me different from all other animals by five this afternoon."

Up jumped Nqa from his bath in the saltpan and shouted, "Go away!"

He was gray and he was woolly, and his pride was inordinate. He danced on a rock-ledge in the middle of Australia and he went to the Middle God Nquing.

He went to Nquing at eight after breakfast, saying, "Make me different from all other animals; make me, also, wonderfully popular by five this afternoon."

59

Up jumped Nquing from his burrow in the spinifex and shouted, "Go away!"

He was gray and he was woolly, and his pride was inordinate. He danced on a sandbank in the middle of Australia and he went to the Big God Nqung.

He went to Nqung at ten before dinnertime, saying, "Make me different from all other animals; make me popular and wonderfully run after by five this afternoon.

Up jumped Nqung from his roost in the Blue Gums and shouted, "Yes, I will!"

Nqung called Dingo — Yellow-Dog Dingo — always hungry, dusty in the sunshine, and showed him Kangaroo. Nqung said, "Dingo! wake up, Dingo! Do you see that gentleman dancing on an ashpit? He wants to be different from all other animals; he wants to be popular and very truly run after. Dingo, make him so!"

Up jumped Dingo — Yellow-Dog Dingo —and said, "What, *that* cat-rabbit?"

Off ran Dingo — Yellow-Dog Dingo — always hungry, grinning like a coal scuttle, and ran after Kangaroo.

Off went the proud Kangaroo on his four little legs like a rabbit. This, oh, Beloved of mine, ends the first part of the tale.

He ran through the desert; he ran through the mountains; he ran through the saltpans; he ran through the reedbeds; he ran through the Blue Gums; he ran through the spinifex. He ran till his front legs ached.

He had to!

Still ran Dingo — Yellow-Dog Dingo — always hungry, grinning like a rattrap, never getting nearer, never getting further.

He had to!

Still ran Kangaroo — Old Man Kangaroo. He ran through the ti-trees; he ran through the mulga; he ran through the long grass; he ran through the short grass; he ran through the Tropics of Capricorn and Cancer. He ran till his hind legs ached.

He had to!

Still ran Dingo — Yellow-Dog Dingo — hungrier and hungrier — grinning like a horse-collar, never getting nearer, never getting further; and they came to the Wollgong River.

Now there wasn't any bridge, and there wasn't any ferryboat, and Kangaroo didn't know how to get over, so he stood on his legs and hopped.

He had to!

He hopped through the Flinders; he hopped through the cinders; he hopped through the deserts in the middle of Australia. He hopped like a Kangaroo.

First he hopped one yard. Then he hopped three yards. Then he hopped five yards; his legs growing stronger; his legs growing longer.

He hadn't any time for rest or refreshment, and he wanted them very much.

Still ran Dingo — Yellow-Dog Dingo — a little bit bewildered, but always hungry, and wondering what in the world or out of it made Old Man Kangaroo hop.

For he hopped like a cricket; like a pea on a gridiron; or a new rubber ball on a nursery floor.

He had to!

He tucked up his front legs; he hopped on his hind legs; he stuck out his tail for a balance-weight behind him; and he hopped through the Darling Downs.

He had to!

Still ran Dingo — Tired-Dog Dingo — hungrier and hungrier, very much bewildered, and wondering when in the world or out of it would Old Man Kangaroo stop.

Then came Nqung from his roost in the Blue Gums and said, "It's five o'clock."

Down sat Dingo — Poor-Dog Dingo — always hungry, dusty in the sunshine and hung out his tongue and howled.

Down sat Kangaroo — Old Man Kangaroo — stuck out his tail like a milking-stool behind him, and said, "Thank goodness *that's* finished!"

Then said Nqung, who is always a gentleman, "Why aren't you grateful to Yellow-Dog Dingo? Why don't you thank him for all he has done for you?"

Then said Kangaroo — tired old Kangaroo — "He's chased me out of the homes of my childhood. He's chased me out of my regular mealtimes. He's altered my shape so I'll never get it back, and he's played Old Scratch with my legs."

Then said Nqung, "Perhaps I'm mistaken, but didn't you ask me to

make you different from all other animals, as well as to make you very truly sought after, by five this afternoon?"

"Yes," said Kangaroo. "I wish now I hadn't. I thought you would do it by charms and incantations, but this is a practical joke."

"Joke!" said Nqung, from his roost in the Blue Gums. "Say that again and I'll whistle up Dingo and run your hind legs off."

"No," said the Kangaroo. "I must apologize; legs are legs and you needn't alter 'em so far as I am concerned. I only meant to explain to Your Lordliness that I've had nothing to eat since morning and I'm very empty indeed."

"Yes," said Dingo — Yellow-Dog Dingo — "I am just in the same situation. I've made him different from all other animals, but what may I have for my tea?"

Then said Nqung from his roost in the Blue Gums, "Come and ask me about it tomorrow, because I'm going to bed."

So they were left in the middle of Australia, Old Man Kangaroo and Yellow-Dog Dingo, and each said, "That's *your* fault."

HOW THE RHINOCEROS GOT HIS WRINKLY SKIN

*Now this is the last tale and it tells how
the Rhinoceros got his wrinkly skin:*

ONCE upon a time, on an uninhabited island on the shores of the Red Sea, there lived a Parsee from whose hat the rays of the sun were reflected in more-than-oriental splendor. And the Parsee lived by the Red Sea with nothing but his hat and a kerosene cooking-stove of the kind that you must particularly never touch. And one day he took flour and water and currants and plums and sugar and things, and made himself one cake which was two feet across and three feet thick. It was indeed a Superior Comestible (*that's* magic), and he put it on the stove because *he* was allowed to cook on that stove, and he baked it and he baked it till it was all done brown and smelled most sentimental. But just as he was going to eat it there came down to the beach from the altogether uninhabited interior one Rhinoceros with a horn on his nose, two piggy eyes, and no manners. In those days the Rhinoceros' skin fitted him quite tight. There were no wrinkles in it anywhere. He looked exactly like a Noah's Ark Rhinoceros, but of course much bigger. All the same, he had no manners then, and he has no manners now, and he never will have any manners. He said, "How!" and the Parsee left that cake and climbed to the top of a palm tree with nothing on but his hat from which the rays of the sun were always reflected in more-than-oriental splendor. And the Rhinoceros upset the oil-stove with his nose, and the cake rolled on the sand, and he spiked that cake on the horn on his nose, and he ate it and he went away, waving his tail, to the desolate and exclusively uninhabited interior which abuts on the islands of Mazanderan, Socotra and the Promontories of the Larger Equinox. Then the Parsee came down from his palm tree and put the stove on its legs and recited the following *Sloka* which as you have not heard I will now proceed to relate:

> Them that take cakes
> Make dreadful mistakes.

And there was a great deal more in that than would meet the Casual Eye!

Because, five weeks later, there was a heat wave in the Red Sea, and everybody took off all the clothes they had. The Parsee took off his hat, but the Rhinoceros took off his skin and carried it over his shoulder as he came down to the beach to bathe. In those days it buttoned up the back with three buttons and looked like a waterproof. He said nothing whatever about the cake because he had eaten it all, and he never had any manners, then, since, or henceforward. He waddled straight into the water and blew bubbles through his nose, leaving his skin on the beach.

Presently the Parsee came by and found the skin, and he smiled one smile that ran all round his face two times. Then he danced three times round the skin and rubbed his hands. Then he went to his camp and filled his hat with cake crumbs — old, dry, stale, tickly cake crumbs, for the Parsee never ate anything but cake, and never swept out his camp. He took that skin, and he shook that skin, and he scrubbed that skin, and he rubbed that skin just as full of old, dry, stale, tickly cake crumbs and some burned currants as ever it could *possibly* hold. Then he climbed to the top of his palm tree and waited for the Rhinoceros to come out of the water and put it on.

And the Rhinoceros did. He buttoned it up the back with three buttons, and it tickled like cake crumbs in bed. Then he wanted to scratch, but that made it worse, and then he lay down on the sands and rolled and rolled and rolled, and every time he rolled the cake crumbs tickled him worse and worse and worse. Then he ran to the palm tree and rubbed and rubbed and rubbed himself against it. He rubbed so much and so hard that he rubbed his skin into a great fold over his shoulders, and another fold over his back where the buttons used to be (but he rubbed the buttons off), and he rubbed some more folds over his legs. And it spoiled his temper, but it didn't make the least difference to the cake crumbs. They were inside his skin and they tickled. So he went home, very angry indeed and horribly scratchy; and from that day to this every rhinoceros has great folds in his skin and a very bad temper, all on account of the cake crumbs inside.

But the Parsee came down from his palm tree, under his hat from which the rays of the sun were reflected in more-than-oriental splendor, packed up the cooking-stove, and went away in the direction of Orotava, Amygdala, the upland meadows of Anantarivo and the marshes of Sonaput — where all small people — beginning to breathe slowly and evenly — must inevitably also accompany him — in order to arrive easily and unknowingly — at the enormous battlements of the luxurious city of Uninterrupted Slumber.

H. B. VESTAL